GENESIS OF THE PHOENIX DAWN

Eternal Grind Book II

Joel Poe

CONTENTS

Chapter 1: Awakening

Amidst the chaotic ruins of an assaulted village, three towering undead trolls thundered their way through the remains, growls reverberating through the once serene air. Joren, Anwar, Lyra, Kolos, and Rafaela – a team stitched together by destiny – stood on a ridge overlooking the scene, their faces resolute.

"Bum!" Lyra yelled at Joren, a smirk playing on her lips despite the grim situation. "Your turn to charm the trolls!"

Joren groaned but stepped forward, steel glinting in his hand as he shifted into his warrior stance. "I swear, Lyra, one of these days..."

The ground shook under the weight of the trolls as Joren dashed into battle, the others following suit. Anwar, his holy armor glinting in the dim light, brandished his sword and charged towards one troll, his courage undeterred by the monstrous creature.

Kolos, the runic mage, was already tracing intricate patterns in the air, his icy-blue eyes focused. As the incantation completed, streaks of arcane energy lashed out, wrapping the second troll in chains of glowing runes.

Lyra, agile and deadly, was a blur of motion. Her twin daggers danced, each move a lethal promise aimed at the third troll. Meanwhile, Rafaela remained slightly behind, her soft hands glowing with warm, healing light.

As the trolls roared, a battle interface popped up before each warrior – a holographic HUD unique to their abilities. Lyra's view buzzed with detailed anatomy points to hit, Rafaela saw the team's health bars, and Anwar's interface glowed with divine seals.

Joren, wielding his blacksmith's hammer, ran headfirst into the troll ensnared by Kolos. A menu popped up, a list of abilities the phoenix warrior could use. He selected "Flaming Strike." His hammer glowed red-hot as he struck, the impact resonating with a fierce battle cry.

Simultaneously, Anwar shouted, "For Aelloria!" The ground beneath him glowed with sacred glyphs, giving him a boost of power as he lunged at his opponent. His blade sliced through the troll, leaving a trail of divine light that seared the undead flesh.

Lyra's knives were a whirlwind, each strike precise and deadly, every move making the most of her rogue skills. She slashed and dodged, her lifebar barely dipping thanks to her agility and Rafaela's support.

Throughout the fight, Rafaela held a constant
stream of healing light, her interface displaying the
team's vitals. Every dip in a health bar had her
sending a surge of healing energy.

The battle was brutal and unforgiving, but their
combined might gradually wore down the trolls.
As the last troll fell, a triumphant cheer erupted
from the villagers who had been watching from a
safe distance.

Their celebration was short-lived, however, as a
dark shadow loomed over the horizon. A bone-
chilling voice echoed across the battlefield, "The
Dark Lord will not be pleased..."

Suddenly, the villagers' joyous laughter turned into
terrified whispers. "The Dark Lord...he's returned."

Lyra turned to Joren, a serious look in her eyes.
"Bum, I think we have more important things to
worry about than charming trolls." She nodded
towards the darkening horizon. "The prophecy...it's
beginning."

As the dark figure loomed closer, Joren looked at his friends, gripping his hammer tighter. "Then let's get ready."

■ ■

Training Module
Ending Simulation in 3...2...1...

Custom Match Disengaged

■ ■

Emerging from the hyper-realistic, immersive training module, a wave of exhaustion washed over Joren, seeping into his bones. His skin was slick with sweat, a result of the intense virtual combat he and his friends had just endured.

Three years they had been grinding, leveling up painstakingly slow, and Joren felt the frustration simmering beneath his stoic exterior.

The sun was setting on the horizon, casting an orange hue over the realm of Aelloria. Despite the world's inherent charm and mystic appeal, Joren could only see the looming shadow of Malazar creeping closer with each passing day. He clenched his fists, the virtual gauntlets flickering out of existence as they disengaged from the module.

"Level 54," he muttered to himself, a scowl pulling at the corners of his lips. It was a reminder of the gap that still existed between them and the tyrant they were meant to overthrow. Even as the Phoenix Warrior, Joren felt the weight of their responsibility resting heavily on his shoulders.

Soft footsteps echoed behind him, and he turned to find Lyra approaching, her digital daggers dissolving into shimmering particles before vanishing entirely. Her azure eyes held a soothing calmness that seemed at odds with the world around them.

"Joren," she began, her voice gentle as a summer breeze. "You're pushing yourself too hard. We all are. We're progressing, just not as quickly as we'd like. We will get stronger."

She took a step closer to him, close enough for him to notice the faint scent of lavender that clung to her, a remnant of the real world seeping into their game-like existence.

"I know it's hard. What happened to Marylynn... It hurts us all. But it's not your fault." Her words were firm, leaving no room for debate. She saw the grief etched in the lines of his face, the guilt that had become his constant companion.

Joren felt a stinging at the back of his eyes, a wetness he quickly blinked away. A man like him didn't cry, couldn't afford to show weakness. But Lyra, with her unwavering gaze and comforting words, stripped him of his armor, leaving him vulnerable.

A single tear slipped past his defenses, leaving a wet trail down his face. It was a quiet testament to his heartache, a silent whisper of his grief. Lyra reached up, her fingers gentle as they brushed the tear away. Her hand lingered, cupping his face as she offered him a sad smile.

"Look at me, Joren," she said softly, her thumb gently stroking his cheek. "I promise you, Malazar will pay for what he's done."

For a moment, there was silence. Only the sound of their breathing echoed between them, a shared rhythm that spoke volumes. They were close, so close that Joren could feel the warmth radiating off her, and for a second, he was lost in her gaze.

They were on the precipice of something new, something uncharted. But just as he was about to lean in, to bridge the gap that had formed between them, a part of him pulled back. It was a wound still fresh, a heartache not yet healed. He withdrew from her touch, stepping back into the familiarity of the friend zone.

"We should head back," he muttered, breaking the spell that had woven itself around them. "Tomorrow's going to be a long day."

A soft blush colored her cheeks as she nodded, stepping away from him. "Right," she said, her voice barely a whisper in the soft breeze. "Let's head back."

As they walked back towards their base, a silence fell between them, heavy with words left unspoken and feelings left unexplored. But for now, they were simply Joren and Lyra - two friends bound by a shared mission, walking the path of heroes under a setting sun.

Chapter 2: The Absence of Fire

Squinting in the early morning sun, Joren looked up at the blue sky. "Fenria," he whispered, "why can't I hear you anymore?" There was no response. Anwar came over, clapping a firm hand on Joren's shoulder.

"Brother, you're overthinking it," Anwar's voice was soft, comforting. "Have some faith. She's there, even if you can't hear her."

A flicker of a smile appeared on Joren's face. "You're the last person I'd expect to hear telling me to have faith, Anwar."

Anwar grinned. "Well, I do surprise myself sometimes."

Their banter was interrupted by the sweet smell of roasting meat. Turning towards the fire, they saw Lyra, expertly turning a spit of rabbit. Her golden hair glowed in the firelight, a sight that never failed to catch Joren's breath.

Kolos was engrossed in a thick tome, muttering to himself. "It's peculiar why Fenria would choose to remain silent now, after all we've been through." He looked up, his blue eyes gleaming with curiosity.

Before Joren could respond, Rafaela chimed in. "Perhaps there's something blocking her voice, something that my healing powers could fix." A brief silence followed Rafaela's proposition, the group absorbing the possibility.

With a collective nod, they agreed. Sitting across Joren, Rafaela closed her eyes, channeling her healing powers. A soft, golden light enveloped her hands as she reached out, her hands hovering over Joren's forehead. A look of concentration crossed her face, her lips moving in a silent prayer.

Minutes passed, the only sound: the crackling of fire. Suddenly, Rafaela recoiled, a gasp escaping her lips. "There's a barrier," she said, her voice filled with disbelief. "A strong one. I can't break through."

"Interesting," Kolos stroked his chin thoughtfully, "very interesting."

Silence fell over the group again. Joren felt a mix of relief and anxiety. He wasn't alone, yet the mystery deepened.

Finally, Anwar broke the silence. "There is one who might have the answers," he said, his voice filled with uncertainty. "The Oracle of Wind Heaven's Peak."

Lyra scoffed, "That's impossible. Even if the Oracle is real, which I highly doubt, no one's seen her in living memory."

A slow smile spread across Kolos's face. "Well, that's where you're wrong, Lyra. I know someone who has..."

Their surprised gasps were drowned by the sudden howl of a wolf in the distance.

Chapter 3: The Howl of Shadows

The howl of the wolf echoed through the forest, chilling their spines. The fire crackled and popped, its light throwing stark, shifting shadows over the surrounding trees. There was something in the way the darkness seemed to drink in the light that made Joren's skin crawl. He rose to his feet, casting his gaze about the edge of their campsite.

"Shadow wolves," Kolos said quietly, rising to his feet and letting his tome slide shut with a snap. The mage's normally playful demeanor was gone, replaced by a grim determination. He moved to stand back-to-back with Joren, his hands glowing with an otherworldly light as he prepared to call upon his magic.

Rafaela was already murmuring prayers under her breath, her hands raised and the faintest shimmer of healing light encasing the party. Anwar, the brave paladin, moved to protect Rafaela, his shield at the ready and his gaze steady on the encroaching darkness.

Lyra, with her agile grace, melted into the

shadows, her twin knives gleaming ominously in the dim light. Her silence was her weapon, and she intended to use it well.

As the growls grew closer, Joren steeled himself. He had his friends beside him, and despite the gnawing absence of Fenria's voice, he had faith. With a shout, he charged at the first shadow wolf that sprang from the darkness.

The creature was massive, a monstrous perversion of nature born of dark magic. Its shadowy form seemed to ripple and shift, making it hard to anticipate its movements. Joren met it with the full force of his fire-infused might, his hammer smashing through the shadowy form, leaving trails of fiery light in its wake.

Anwar and Kolos worked in tandem, Anwar drawing the attention of two more shadow wolves while Kolos bombarded them with his spells. The air crackled with energy as the mage let loose, his words of power shaping reality around them.

Rafaela focused her powers on maintaining the protective shield around them, ensuring that no stray shadow wolves could penetrate their defensive line. Every now and then, she directed a beam of healing light towards Joren or Anwar, mending their injuries and reinforcing their stamina.

And then there was Lyra. Like a ghost, she moved through the shadows, striking with deadly accuracy. The wolves barely had time to react before she was gone, lost in the darkness once again.

After what seemed like hours, the growls and howls started to fade. One by one, the shadow wolves dissipated into nothingness, their forms dispersing into the night. The party, bruised but unbeaten, took a collective breath, their senses still on high alert.

"That was a close one," Joren grunted falling back onto a log, his body aching from the intense fight. The others nodded, returning to the dying embers of the campfire, the peace of their meal shattered by the unexpected ambush.

"Shadow wolves don't usually hunt in packs like this," Kolos mused aloud, his brows furrowed in thought. "Especially not this far from Malazar's territory."

"Could Malazar be expanding his influence?" Anwar asked, concern creasing his brows.

Before anyone could respond, a loud crack echoed through the air. Suddenly, the ground beneath them started to quake, and a massive, gnarled tree nearby began to uproot itself, its eyes glowing with the same shadowy energy as the wolves.

It was not just a pack of shadow wolves they had to contend with, but a Shadow Elder Tree, a far more formidable opponent, and it was headed right their way.

Chapter 4: The Elder Tree

Joren stood at the vanguard, his resolve firm as iron. The immense Elder Tree towered over them, its eyes ablaze with the familiar sinister shadow energy they had seen in the wolves. The very air trembled under the weight of its wrath, but Joren stood unflinching, the absence of Fenria's voice momentarily forgotten as he girded himself for the impending battle.

Anwar stood beside him in an instant, holy light radiating around him, an aurora of faith forming a shield. Kolos, the mage, began whispering incantations, his hands dancing through the air, sketching runes as he prepared his spells. Rafaela, the healer, was close to Kolos, her hands glowing with the calming radiance of her healing magic. Lyra, the stealthy rogue, had once again vanished into the shadows, her knives gleaming in the intermittent moonlight.

Yet, before they could strike or shield themselves, a resonant voice echoed through the forest, the words heavy and ancient, shaking the earth beneath them. It was the Elder Tree, speaking in an archaic dialect, the words oddly soothing and musical despite the shadow-twisted form looming above them.

"Hold thy weapons, noble warriors! Methinks mine self is not thy foe. 'Tis Malazar's foul magic that clouds mine judgment and stirs mine fury."

The Elder Tree's plea bore a certain authenticity. Joren found himself lowering his hammer, his gaze still warily fixed on the colossal creature.

"Tell us how we can free you of Malazar's influence?" he asked, addressing the Elder Tree.

"Through unity and light, a harmonious blend of thy powers," the Elder Tree replied. "Innocence must lead, the light bearer must follow, wit and agility shall confound, and fire shall cleanse."

Anwar and Rafaela exchanged a knowing glance, a silent understanding passing between them. Anwar, as the embodiment of innocence, was the first to step forward. He placed a hand on the gnarled bark of the Elder Tree, channeling his purest intentions. Rafaela, the light bearer, followed, her healing magic flooding into the Elder Tree, seeking out the dark corruption.

Lyra and Kolos, representing agility and wit respectively, employed their skills to befuddle the dark magic. Lyra's swift movements and Kolos's cunning spells ran rings around Malazar's lingering influence, disrupting its grip and creating openings for Joren.

Lastly, Joren stepped forth, his phoenix fire imbuing his hammer with a warm, cleansing glow. This was not the fire of destruction, but of rebirth. He struck the Elder Tree, the fiery essence from his hammer eating away at the dark magic plaguing the ancient being.

Under their relentless onslaught, the shadowy influence writhed, struggled, but eventually began to wane. With a final, decisive strike, Joren slammed his hammer into the Elder Tree's massive trunk. There was a brilliant flash of light, followed by a silence that hung heavy in the air.

As the light receded, they saw the Elder Tree, now free from the dark magic. It stood tall, its eyes filled with the age-old wisdom of the forest, a serene green aura replacing the foreboding darkness. The Elder Tree seemed more vibrant, its bark now a healthy brown, untouched by corruption.

"Verily, I owe thee mine life, noble warriors. I am in thy debt," the Elder Tree expressed, its form bowing in a graceful arch.

"We're just glad we could help," Joren replied, resting his hammer on his shoulder. "But tell us, how did Malazar control you, an ancient and powerful being?"

The Elder Tree's eyes hardened, and a sigh-like breeze rustled through its leaves. It was gathering its thoughts, preparing to share a tale that would likely send a chill down their spines.

Chapter 5:
Deathreaver

Gathered beneath the expansive branches of the newly cleansed Elder Tree, the party listened with rapt attention, their faces alight with anticipation and trepidation. The giant's deep voice began to weave the tale, its old, creaky timbre making the words seem even more profound.

"Verily," he started, his voice echoing around the silent woods, "The Deathreaver, an artifact of unspeakable dread and calamity, hath been hidden in the sands of time. Pilfered from the very clutches of Death herself by the first Shadow Monarch, its name doth instill fear in the hearts of mortals and immortals alike. To wield such a scepter is to master Death herself."

Kolos' magical codex fluttered open, its ethereal pages whirling in the air, reflecting the flickering firelight. The ancient words and symbols seemed to dance as he echoed the Elder Tree's explanation.

"Aye," he said, "To possess Deathreaver, 'tis said, is to rule over death and life."

The group exchanged puzzled looks. The artifact sounded like a fable, a grim tale told to scare children. How could they be certain that such a thing truly existed, and that it was not merely another one of Malazar's machinations to instill fear?

In response, the ancient Elder Tree gave a sorrowful sigh that rustled the leaves around them. He looked down upon them, his ancient eyes filled with a knowing sadness. "Alas," he said, "for I have seen the woe it brings upon the world. I know of its existence and the terrible power it confers upon its holder."

As they watched the Elder Tree prepare to weave the tale of the Deathreaver, the fire crackled and the wind whistled through the trees.
The Elder Tree's slow, haunting voice echoing in their ears, "Allow me to enlighten thee about the origins and the horror of the Deathreaver..."

Chapter 6: The Elder's Burden

The moonlight wove a silver tapestry through the leaves above, as the Elder Tree commenced his tale of the infamous Deathreaver. His voice, haunting yet captivating, filled the air, and the rustling of the leaves seemed to echo his somber tones.

"In times of yore," he began, "the Deathreaver was entrusted to our kindred, the noble Elder Trees. Bound to the pulse of the earth, we cherish the cycle of life and respect the balance of mortality. We crave not the mastery of death, but honor the marvel of life in all its forms."

"Thus, the Deathreaver was secreted in the heart of our sanctuary, hidden from those who sought its destructive potential. But Malazar, the vile serpent, had been weaving his web of deceit, casting his malevolent gaze upon the forest for centuries. He sought to claim what was not his, to warp the essence of life and death."

As the ancient creature continued his tale, his eyes gleamed with a mixture of sadness and fear. "Perhaps, one of our own betrayed us, drawn to the whispers of power, or perhaps Malazar himself unravelled the secrets of our sanctuary. The truth remains obscured, but the consequence is clear; the scepter is in his grasp."

With the revelation hanging heavy in the air, the Elder Tree then turned his gaze to Joren, his eyes filled with wisdom and the weight of centuries. "He seeks thee, Phoenix Warrior," he intoned, his voice deep and steady. "The flame within thee is the only beacon of hope that remains. The only force that can oppose the coming darkness."

Joren, taken aback by the sudden address, could only stare at the Elder Tree in silent wonder. The great creature had seen through him, recognized the burgeoning power within him. The realization was both humbling and alarming.

As the wind whispered through the trees and the fire crackled in the silence, Joren's mind raced. The magnitude of his destiny was becoming clearer with each passing moment. He was not just a blacksmith or a warrior, but a beacon of hope, the Phoenix Warrior, standing against the encroaching darkness.

Joel Poe

Chapter 7: The Last Stand

As the moon bathed the clearing in its somber light, Joren unburdened his fears and doubts to the wise Elder Tree. His voice echoed amidst the ancient trunks, revealing his anguish over Fenria's silence.

The wise Elder Tree listened attentively, his eyes glinting with understanding. "Oftentimes," he rumbled, "what we seek is hidden not in the depths of uncertainty, but in the light of plain sight. Trust in thyself, young Phoenix Warrior, and trust in the bond thou sharest with Fenria. She hath not abandoned thee without purpose. Time shall reveal the reason."

Their conversation was abruptly halted by the sound of distant horns, ominous growls, and dreadful, thunderous steps. The peace of the clearing was shattered, replaced by an eerie tension.

Emerging from the shadows, Lyra appeared, her face graver than usual. "An army of the undead is approaching," she warned, her voice strained.

"They have an Undertaker with them."

A quest prompt materialized on the Elder Tree's User HUD Display. "Quest Name: It's too late for me." Two options appeared below it: "Accept Quest" and "Ignore Quest". Joren glanced at the display, his heart hammering in his chest.

The Elder Tree gently touched the Accept Quest button with his gnarled fingers. "Fear not, young ones," he addressed them. "May the winds of nature be always on thy back."

With his last farewell, the Elder Tree turned towards the approaching horde. "It is time for me to return to the soil from whence I came," he declared. Despite Joren's protests, the Elder Tree insisted, his resolve unyielding.

Our heroes fled the scene, their hearts heavy with dread and gratitude. Behind them, they could hear the sounds of the battle ensuing, the defiant roars of the brave Elder Tree against the ceaseless onslaught.

Their last glimpse of the ancient guardian was him standing tall and resilient, an embodiment of natural fury against the wave of decay. His sacrifice allowed them to escape, his last stand a testament to the unyielding spirit of nature.

And so fell the mighty guardian, his life given to secure a chance at hope for the young Phoenix Warrior and his companions.

Chapter 8: The Dark Lord's Ire

Within the grim fortress of Wraith Spire, an unsettling tension brooded. Born of black obsidian and formidable death magic, the stronghold seemed to breathe an eerie life of its own. It whispered tales of dread and doom, its icy halls echoing with the chilling crackle of the unholy flames flickering in the braziers.

Deep in this stronghold, Malazar, the Dark Lord, paced like a restless storm. His skeletal fingers tapped rhythmically against the throne of bone and obsidian, a morbid symphony to his growing ire. His rage simmered beneath the surface, radiating an aura of palpable menace.

The cacophony of hushed whispers and fluttering wings announced the arrival of the Harpies. Their voices, a shrill chorus, cut through the spectral silence with news of the Phoenix Warrior.

"My Lord," began the bravest of the Harpies, her voice an uneasy blend of respect and fear, "the Phoenix Warrior has eluded our grasp once again."

Malazar's response was a low growl, simmering with repressed rage. His blazing eyes bore into the Harpy, making her quiver. "How can a mere boy evade you time and again?" he thundered, his voice reverberating through the chilled stone of his fortress.

The second Harpy hesitated before speaking, her voice trembling slightly, "An Elder Tree, my Lord, more resilient than anticipated, interfered with our plans."

Malazar's rage erupted, his fury filling the echoing halls of the Spire. "Inefficiency and incompetence!" he spat. The fortress seemed to shudder at his wrath, the eternal flames flickering in response.

Amid the mounting tension, the third Harpy stepped forward, an air of terror surrounding her. "Send me, Lord Malazar," she suggested, her voice laced with anticipation. "I shall not disappoint you."

The Dark Lord scrutinized her, his cold gaze paralyzing. A moment of silence hung in the air, ominous and heavy. Finally, he spoke, "You had better not...or the consequences will be far graver than you can comprehend." The harpy swallowed hard. With a nod of acceptance, she left the gathering, her mission set before her.

Chapter 9: An Unseen Source

Night blanketed the forest with a mantle of obsidian stars. Our heroes, worn and weary, trudged along, their boots crunching on a carpet of dried leaves. Lyra's keen eyes found them a refuge for the night: a deep, hidden cave promising shelter and secrecy.

They agreed to her plan, desperate for rest. Once inside, Joren ignited a small, contained fire, its warm glow dancing upon their weary faces. The smoke from the fire spiraled upward, escaping through a tiny fissure in the cave roof, while the warmth remained, a much-needed respite against the chill of the night.

As they settled in, Rafaela knelt beside Anwar, her delicate fingers lightly brushing over his twisted ankle. He winced at the touch, but her soothing aura began to knit the pain away. On the sideline, Kolos watched, his brows knitted in silent frustration. No words passed his lips, but jealousy was clearly gnawing at him.

"We're running out of soal stones," Rafaela noted, her attention shifting back to the task at hand. "We need to replenish our mana supplies soon."

Kolos nodded, his mind working through the logistics. "We have to find a way to gather some. The next phase of our journey demands it."

Anwar, leaning against the cave wall, offered a smirk. "Who needs soal stones when we have our very own Phoenix Warrior? Isn't his fire unending, unquenchable, undying?"

Lyra chimed in, her voice soft in the dim light. "I feel it too, you know. A force so close, yet out of our reach. It's like we're swimming in his power but don't have the permit to use it."

Kolos, ever the strategist, tapped his chin thoughtfully. "Could it be that we can harness Joren's power?" He turned to Joren. "Could you allow us access to your mana?"

Joren sighed, the fire reflecting in his eyes. "If I knew how, I would. But without Fenria, I don't know how to control or share this... power."

The air seemed to shimmer with expectation, awaiting Kolos's response. He smiled then, his eyes twinkling with a secret. "I know someone who might be able to help us with that."

Rafaela perked up, interest piqued. "Who?" she asked, her voice echoing the intrigue of the rest.

Kolos's smile broadened. "The very person who has seen the Oracle in living memory."

The news hung heavy in the air, like a promise of hope and a portent of the challenges yet to come.

Chapter 10: Out of the Frying Pan

In the heart of the cave, the cold chill of a looming threat sent shivers down their spines. The distant echo of a harpy's shriek cut through the night air, causing a momentary pause in their conversation. The cozy cave suddenly felt less secure and more like a trap.

"Put out the fire, now!" Lyra ordered in a hushed voice, her eyes glowing eerily in the darkened cave. The rogue was the first to sense the approaching danger.

Rafaela turned to Kolos, her usually calm face showing a rare hint of fear. "Can you teleport us out of here?" she asked, her hands already reaching for her small stash of soal stones. Her eyes were on Anwar, the holy paladin, standing resolute, his hand already gripping the hilt of his sword, the gleaming shield slung across his back adding a semblance of security to their predicament.

Kolos didn't answer immediately, his gaze distant

as he pondered their situation. "There's a risk," he admitted. "With the scant soal stones we have left, I might not control where we reappear."

Anwar stepped in, his voice firm despite the imminent danger. "A risk we must take. We're not equipped to face a harpy, not in our current condition."

The group collectively nodded. As much as they wanted to fight, they understood the wisdom of Anwar's words. "I need time," Kolos declared, his fingers already sparking with the early beginnings of an incantation. "I need about 3 minutes."

Rafaela's eyes went wide. "That's a long time."

Kolos nodded, understanding the gravity of the situation. "I know, but a harpy is drawn to mana. She'll sense the incantation."

"Well," Lyra said, drawing her twin daggers, the blade edges gleaming ominously in the dim light, "Then we better give her something else to focus on."

Joren, the Phoenix Warrior, tightened his grip on his hammer. The embers of the dying fire reflected in his eyes, mirroring the fire of resolve in his heart.

They readied themselves, prepared to buy Kolos the precious time he needed, even as the harpy's screeching grew closer, her lethal presence casting a deadly shadow over the cave's entrance. The embers in the fire pit died, plunging the cave into a tense darkness, the silence disrupted only by the distant echo of the harpy's haunting cry.

Chapter 11: The Harpy's Dance

The howling of the wind and the harpy's shrill cries filled the air as the cave entrance was bathed in the creature's ghastly glow. Level 77, a formidable opponent. The harpy was a haunting silhouette against the night sky, its wings flapping menacingly as it descended onto them.

"Rafaela, Anwar, front-line defense. Lyra, keep her wings clipped. Joren, be ready to cover us if we falter," Kolos ordered, his gaze not leaving the creature as he began to chant in an ancient language, his hands tracing complex patterns in the air.

Anwar brandished his sword, the blessed blade gleaming in the darkness. His shield was raised, ready to defend against the harpy's talons. Beside him, Rafaela's hands shimmered with greenish energy, the remnants of her mana reserves aiding in her healing and defensive enchantments.

Lyra, with her twin daggers, darted towards the creature, her stealth aiding her in her task. A faint flicker of light and she was gone, the harpy suddenly squawking as a dagger hit one of its wings, limiting its flight.

Joren held his position, hammer gripped tightly, molten fire stirring within him. His eyes were on the portal Kolos was desperately trying to create, the incantation causing the air to waver, a rip in reality slowly forming.

The battle was fierce. Anwar and Rafaela held the front, their coordinated defense keeping the harpy at bay. Lyra's blades flashed in and out of sight, a constant distraction for the beast. And above it all, Kolos' chanting echoed, a testament to their desperate hope.

The final moments were a rush. The harpy, frustrated and enraged, screeched and lunged towards the distracted Kolos, the portal just about stable. In a heartbeat, Joren was there, the Phoenix Warrior coming to life in a blaze of glory.

"Molten Hammer!" He roared, a shroud of brilliant fire enveloping him as he charged the harpy. His weapon clashed against the creature, snaring it in a flaming trap, buying them those precious seconds. The party didn't wait, rushing towards the portal.

"Go!" Joren ordered, his strength holding the beast back as his friends disappeared through the portal.

Finally, with a last burst of courage, Joren disengaged, sprinting towards the wavering portal. The harpy, free from his snare, shrieked in fury, lunging after him. But it was a moment too late. Joren plunged into the portal, his figure blurring and then disappearing, the portal closing behind him just as the harpy's talons swiped the space where he had been moments ago. The cave fell into silence, the echoes of battle lingering in the chilled night air.

Chapter 12: Echoes of a Whisper

Their reprieve was short-lived. The ethereal calm of their new surrounding was shattered when Kolos collapsed to the ground, blood staining his lips a chilling crimson.

"Is anyone hurt?" Rafaela asked, her voice echoing through the strange expanse they found themselves in. But her healer's senses alerted her to the truth even before the words left her mouth.

The party rushed towards Kolos, forming a protective circle around their fallen friend. Rafaela kneeled, her hands faintly glowing as she tried to assess the extent of his injuries. The glow faltered, sputtered and died out.

"Internal bleeding... he has drained himself of mana... and beyond," she said, her voice trembling.

Lyra knelt beside her, her usual stoic demeanor replaced with fear. "But how... He couldn't cast without mana..."

"Unless..." Anwar began, his voice faltering.

Rafaela finished for him, her words barely a whisper. "Blood magic."

Joren, feeling the shock ripple through their group, asked what she meant.

Anwar explained, his voice heavy with sorrow. "Blood magic... it's a form of magic where the user sacrifices their health in exchange for mana. It's a dangerous, desperate measure. The user can cast spells for as long as they can endure the damage... until..."

"Until they die," Rafaela added, her hands still hovering over Kolos, her healing power not even enough to mend a simple cut now.

Their words hung heavy in the air, silence stretching into a painful eternity. Joren, stricken, knelt beside Kolos. He could not let another friend fall, not when he had the power to help. But how?

With a raw cry, he called for Fenria. He called for

her, pleaded, demanded for her guidance. His
voice echoed, each shout an unanswered plea.
Then, just when he was about to surrender to the
harsh reality, he heard it. A faint voice, a whisper
on the wind. His heart skipped a beat.

"Fenria? Is that you?" His voice was a mix of hope
and despair. He demanded to know why she had
left him, especially now when they needed her the
most. "My friend is dying, Fenria. We need your
help. Tell me what I must do..." His voice trailed
off, the silence swallowing his words.

His plea echoed in the vast expanse, a last plea for
a dying friend. They waited, held their breaths, and
hoped against hope for an answer.

Chapter 13: End of Tutorial

Joren was no longer standing in the strange, eerie plane. Instead, he found himself surrounded by a serenity unlike any other. A tranquil realm of silvery trees, shining waters, a place too pristine and serene to be real. At the heart of it all, a lake of shimmering blue fire, a flame that didn't burn, bathed the place in a soft, soothing glow. A faint light flickered at the center, dimming with every passing second.

"Fenria?" His voice echoed across the ethereal landscape. "What's happening?"

Her response was as faint as the dying light. "Joren, we have little time. My journey with you is nearing its end. The upload process... it's almost complete. I won't be able to take a separate form anymore. I'm merging with you."

Confusion etched on his face, Joren asked, "Then why can't I see you? Why can't I feel your wisdom?"

Fenria's voice remained calm amidst his flurry of

questions. "You must look deeper. The knowledge I hold is yours too. You have the power to save your friend. But you must connect with the Phoenix Force. I can no longer act as a mediator. I cannot speak for her any further."

His heart pounded in his chest. All this time, he had believed Fenria to be the Phoenix. But she was not? She was merely a conduit, a representative?

"No one is ever ready," she continued, her light waning even further. "But we do what we must with what we're given. I am always with you, a part of you. You don't need me anymore." Suddenly, a notification popped up on his screen.

End of Tutorial

---

it read, with an 'Accept' button below it. No option to decline. He was taken aback, uncertainty making his heart heavy. The countdown appeared, ticking away the seconds.

"Your friends need you, Joren," Fenria whispered,

the last of her light fading away. "Tutorial mode deactivated."

Joren jerked awake, pulled back from the tranquil plane to the harsh reality. He realized that no time had passed in the real world, even though it felt like he had spent hours in the other realm.

Lyra's voice broke his reverie. "Joren, are you okay?" Her eyes bore into him, concern etched on her face.

He turned to look at her, a newfound determination in his gaze.

Chapter 14: Tears of the Phoenix

Rafaela's sobbing echoed through the eerie silence. Her desperate pleas for Kolos' life hung heavily in the air as each of the companions wrestled with their own helplessness. The mage lay dying on the cold, hard ground. His life force was diminishing, and they all could feel it.

Joren, however, seemed different. The normally boisterous blacksmith was calm, his fiery spirit quelled into a serene stillness that contrasted sharply with the chaos around him. He knelt by Kolos' side, placing a comforting hand on Rafaela's trembling shoulder. His calm demeanor brought an air of solace to the distraught healer.

"Reach out, whatever is in me, I give to you," he implored, his gaze meeting Rafaela's. His words held a certain conviction, an unquestionable faith in his newfound understanding of his phoenix abilities.

"But how?" Rafaela faltered, the confusion evident in her eyes.

"Just do it, Rafaela," Joren reassured, unbuttoning his robe to reveal his bare chest. His heart was visible beneath his skin, beating steadily. He guided her hands to it, a gesture of trust and unity. "Here."

And so, Rafaela did as told. With her hands over his heart, she closed her eyes and reached out to the energy within him. Joren did the same, seeking out the unknown depths of the phoenix power that resided within his being.

A sense of urgency pushed him to plead with the silent force within him. "Whatever fire you've given me," he urged inwardly, "pass it down to my friend. Let me die if I must. But save him, please."

For a few agonizing moments, nothing happened. But then, something miraculous occurred. A single tear, glowing with a bright blue flame, slid down Joren's cheek and fell onto Rafaela's forearm. The sight of it drew gasps from everyone present, a beacon of hope in the midst of despair.

A new prompt flashed on Joren's HUD: "Ability Unlocked: Tears of the Phoenix," it read, with the description tab revealing, "Tears of the Phoenix: Replenish your ally's mana. Cooldown 48 hours. Can be upgraded into Blood of the Phoenix. Level required to use Blood of the Phoenix: Information Unavailable for Public Disclosure."

As the knowledge of his new ability seeped into Joren's consciousness, a new energy surged within Rafaela. The blue fire from Joren's tear infused her with an incredible surge of mana. Her eyes glowed an intense green, reminiscent of a fresh sprout bursting from the earth. Her mana bar overflowed, the screen glowing with power.

"It worked!" Anwar exclaimed, eyes wide with astonishment. "He did it!"

Lyra looked on, awed by Joren's transformation. The young man she had known was rapidly evolving, shouldering the weight of his newfound abilities with a courage that was inspiring.

With a newfound strength, Rafaela turned her attention back to Kolos. Both her hands rested gently on the mage, ready to channel the healing energy coursing within her. As they all held their breath, she began.

Chapter 15: The Stag's Arrival

As Rafaela channeled her newfound strength into Kolos, everyone watched with bated breath. Slowly but surely, Kolos' eyes flickered open, and a small, weak grin appeared on his face. The relief that washed over Rafaela was immense, and without a second thought, she pulled him into a tight hug.

Tears of joy streaked down her face as she buried her face in his shoulder. Kolos chuckled softly, his voice weak but teasing, "Well, I didn't know you cared so much, Rafaela."

A blush tinted Rafaela's cheeks as she pulled back, realizing that she had just revealed a part of her heart that she had kept hidden. But there was no time for embarrassment; their friend was alive, and that was all that mattered.

Rafaela looked at Kolos seriously, her eyes brimming with unshed tears, "Promise me, Kolos. Promise me you'll never do something like this again. If anything were to happen to you, I..."

"Guys, we got company," Lyra's voice cut through the emotional reunion, snapping everyone back into the present.

They all turned to see a great stag approaching them. It was easily the biggest stag they had ever seen, standing at least nine feet tall, its antlers branching out like an intricate, regal crown. The majestic creature walked towards them with a slow, dignified grace, its large eyes looking at them curiously.

Joren's hand hovered over his weapon, the past experiences making him wary of unexpected appearances. Was this a friend or foe? The stag seemed calm and not at all aggressive, but the group had learned that appearances could be deceiving.

His eyes met the stag's, a silent question hanging in the air. Should they prepare for a fight, or should they run?

Chapter 16: Blessing of the Great Stag

Anwar, without a moment of hesitation, dropped his sword and shield, his protective armor clattering against the ground. He approached the great stag and knelt before it. The stag breathed onto the paladin, and a sense of peace and revitalization filled Anwar's body. His tired and worn-out features seemed to brighten.

Joren, always wary, observed the stag through his HUD. It registered the stag's level as "Unspecified" and classified it as a "Deity," with an element noted as the "Power of Will." He frowned, puzzled. How could *will* be an *element*?

Kolos, leaning on Rafaela for support, hobbled over to Joren. "Joren, lower your weapon. This stag means us no harm. If it intended otherwise, we would stand no chance against such a powerful entity."

With that, Kolos and Rafaela walked past Joren
and knelt beside Anwar. Lyra followed suit,
leaving Joren as the only one standing, his hand
still gripping his weapon tightly.

The stag turned its gaze to Joren, its eyes meeting
his. A wave of intense emotion washed over Joren,
his body unable to move, yet it wasn't fear that
held him captive. It was an overwhelming sense of
love and connection. The stag's gaze seemed to
pierce his soul, recognizing him as a long-lost
friend.

Joren found himself walking towards the stag, not
in the form of a challenge, but rather of
acceptance. He reached out, and rather than
kneeling like the others, he hugged the creature.
The stag breathed onto him, and a message
appeared on his HUD, "Blessing of Will: Bonus
50% Experience Gained for the next 72 hours."

The moment felt like a reunion, an echo of a bond
that had existed long before he could remember.

The stag met his gaze once more, seeming to say, "It was good to see you, old friend." Joren was uncertain if the sentiment was meant for him or if the stag was recognizing the Phoenix within him. After all, it was a deity acknowledging another, the stag and the Phoenix, friends across ages past.

As the stag slowly retreated, a new calmness swept over the group. They had received a blessing, a gift of Will, from an ancient deity, filling them with hope for the challenges to come.

Chapter 17: Arrival at Wind Heaven's Peak

The group still reverberated from the encounter with the stag. Joren was perplexed, not knowing what to make of this intense feeling of love that he felt for the deity. "What just happened? Who or what was that? Why do I feel so...connected to it?" he asked the group.

Anwar was the first to respond. "That was the Spirit of Will, a god from the ancient world. It's one of the few deities that remains. It is said to only appear before those who refuse to back down, regardless of the odds stacked against them."

Kolos added, "Being a deity of the old world, it would've felt your presence from worlds away, Joren. With both you and the stag being forces of good that have kept the world in balance for millennia, it's no wonder the two of you recognized each other."

Rafaela nodded in agreement, adding her own perspective as an empath. "I could feel the emotions radiating from both the Stag and from within Joren. There was a sense of mutual respect, of care, of sorrow."

Kolos then brought the conversation back to their current predicament. "We need to figure out where we are. Does anyone have a map?" Lyra shrugged, indicating she had no clues.

Anwar was lost in his thoughts, staring at a distant mountain range covered in clouds. "Anwar! Anwar! Are you okay?" Joren asked, breaking his silence. Anwar simply pointed towards the towering mountains, a marvel that they hadn't noticed until now.

Walking alongside Anwar, the group came to a stop as they too took in the magnificent view. Kolos, in awe, whispered, "Wind Heaven's Peak..."

Rafaela continued, her voice barely audible, "We

are...here... I dare not believe it."

"Here? Where is 'here'? Where are we?" asked a confused Joren. Lyra teased him, "You really can be dense sometimes, Bum. Don't you see? We're on..."

Anwar finished her sentence, his voice filled with a mix of awe and disbelief, "The mystic land of the Great Oracle."

Chapter 18: Level Up

Suddenly, Joren's HUD lit up once again. "Achievement Unlocked: Discovering the Land of the Gods" it read. Instantly, the entire party leveled up. Due to the Blessing of Will that Joren received from the stag, everyone benefited from an experience bonus as they were all in the same party.

They were now around level 57, an impressive leap forward. Each member of the party quickly went about choosing new abilities and investing their newly earned talent points. Rafaela, Kolos, Anwar, and Lyra dove into their respective healing, arcane, holy paladin, and rogue trees, while Joren looked through his own.

Anwar was unsure about his choices, "Guys, should I go full defense?" he asked. Joren was too engrossed in his own skill tree to offer much advice, but he managed a quick, "Up to you."

"Oh!" Kolos exclaimed excitedly, "I've always wanted this ability! Blast Arcane Maxima!"

Lyra, on the other hand, was delving into her poison tree. She unlocked the ability for her weapons to be automatically infused with poison and added a new skill, Grievous Wounds, that would cause additional bleeding damage.

Rafaela, while still focusing on her healing abilities, decided to branch out a bit into the druidic healing tree. This gave her the power to dispel malevolent curses and administer antidotes for poisons in the heat of combat.

Joren, unlike the others, had no choice in his new ability. The only option he was given was to accept. It was an ability named Fists of the Phoenix, a hand-to-hand combat skill that would set his fists ablaze. He pondered over this new ability, conflicted. He'd always been a hammer-wielder, from his blacksmith days to his current warrior lifestyle. This new skill contradicted everything he knew about his own style of fighting.

"Everybody good? You picked your talents and abilities?" Joren asked, pulling everyone out of their individual reveries. Each one of them confirmed that they had made their choices.

"So, what's the plan now?" asked Joren, seeking direction for their next move.

"I went full defense, guys!" Anwar blurted out, showing his excitement about his new abilities.

Chapter 19: The Storm Fox

With their newly acquired abilities, the team now faced the task of planning their next move. Kolos voiced his suspicion that their arrival at this location was far from coincidental. If the portal had brought them here, it was probably because some higher power intended for them to find this place.

Anwar supported this notion. "Agreed," he said. "We should go up the mountains, find the Great Oracle, like I said before."

Lyra interrupted him, "Weren't you listening the first time? No one has ever made it up there. And if they did, they certainly never came back. It's not even known whether the Oracle is still there... For all we know, it may never have been there to begin with..."

Kolos interjected, "That's not entirely accurate. There is one person who has been up there, in fact, and has seen the Oracle."

Curious, Joren inquired, "Who are you referring to?"

Kolos hesitated for a moment, as if lost in his own

thoughts. "The Storm Fox," he finally uttered.

Rafaela was taken aback. "You mean the great Antonius?" she asked, her tone carrying a note of incredulity.

Lyra chimed in, her voice full of disbelief. "Wait... you seriously don't mean..."

Kolos nodded, interrupting her. "Yes," he said with a solemnity that silenced them all. "The old man... Silverhand himself." He paused, his eyes far away. "My mentor."

Chapter 20: Path to the Oracle

They had reached an impasse, standing before the mammoth challenge that was Wind Heaven's Peak. Joren turned to Kolos, a befuddled look etched across his face, "Why didn't you say anything earlier?"

Kolos, quick to infuse some of his characteristic humor into the tension-thick air, playfully rolled his eyes, "Oh, I'm sorry, was I supposed to provide a detailed itinerary whilst being mauled by a Harpy and fighting to keep my lifeblood in its rightful place? My sincerest apologies!"

Despite the gravity of their circumstances, Joren couldn't help but chuckle at his friend's biting sarcasm. "Fair point, Kolos," he conceded, the gravity of their conversation momentarily lifted. Lyra, ever the pragmatic one, brought their focus back to the matter at hand. "Okay, enough jesting," she insisted, "How do we get up that behemoth of a mountain? Can it be climbed? Should I start flexing my biceps in preparation?"

Kolos, shedding his jester's mask for a moment, replied in a grave tone, "Well, certainly, teleportation is out of the question. The peak is entirely sealed. No one gets in or out through magical means, thanks to a persistent anti-magic barrier."

Anwar, brows knitted together in confusion, interjected, "And how do you know all of this, again? Did you get an insider's tip from a mountain goat?"

Kolos face-palmed dramatically, groaning in exasperation, "For the love of - my master has been there! How many times do I have to play this broken record?"

Chagrined, Anwar raised his hands in surrender, "Alright, alright, no need to pop a vein, Kolos."

"So," Joren interrupted, trying to steer the

conversation back on track, "we climb, then?" Lyra squinted at him skeptically, "Are you out of your mind, or is this another side effect of becoming the phoenix's chosen?"

"No, he's right," Kolos backed Joren up, adding, "There really is no other way. Plus, let's not forget, we'll be dealing with an assortment of delightful obstacles custom-made to test anyone daring enough to seek the Oracle. They really like to roll out the welcome mat up there."

Rafaela chimed in, her voice steady, "If we are to succeed, then we must unite as one, look out for each other. This isn't a leisurely stroll through a meadow."

"I couldn't agree more," Anwar said, his earlier joviality replaced by resolve. Lyra nodded in silent agreement, her gaze set firmly on the daunting mountain before them.

Joren took a deep breath, looking at each of his companions in turn. "We're all in agreement then," he said, a steely determination in his voice. "We go up Wind Heaven's Peak... come what may."

"And if there's a souvenir shop at the top, I call dibs on a snow globe!" Kolos chimed in, unable to resist adding a touch of levity to their monumental decision.

Chapter 21: The Game is Afoot

Deep within the obsidian walls of his fortress, the Dark Lord Malazar brooded over his latest setback. The cold, echoing throne room was lit solely by the eerie glow emanating from the dreaded Deathreaver Scepter, casting an ominous pallor on his pale, grim face.

The screeching entrance of the Harpy shattered the silence, her form haggard, battered and bloodied, a testament to the fierce resistance she had encountered at the cave. Malazar's gaze fixed on her with a menacing intensity, a wordless demand for an explanation.

"The Phoenix Warrior," she stammered, her voice shrill with trepidation, "He escaped... again."

Malazar's enraged roar echoed through the stone halls of the fortress, a dreadful symphony of fury and frustration. His power swelled around him like a tempest, his control over the elements a terrifying spectacle. He raised the Deathreaver Scepter, its deadly tip poised to strike the trembling Harpy, his face a mask of cold, ruthless fury.

Yet, as the Scepter descended, the Harpy mustered her final ounce of courage, crying out, "I know where they teleported!"

The Scepter halted, mere inches from her vulnerable flesh. Malazar, his dark power ebbing, met her fearful gaze with his own penetrating one. "Speak," he demanded, his voice an icy whisper.

Shivering under the weight of his gaze, the Harpy dared to share her secret, "Wind Heaven's Peak, Lord."

A heavy silence fell over the throne room as Malazar absorbed the words. Wind Heaven's Peak. The land of the old gods, a place as revered as it was feared. A location he knew too well from his past.

If the Phoenix Warrior had indeed taken refuge there, it could mean only one thing: help was at hand. A particular help, from a man he loathed above all others in Aelloria. The name slipped from his lips, its very mention a bitter taste in his mouth, "Antonius Silverhand."

His old nemesis. His rival. His former friend. It seemed that the gods had a sense of humor, forcing him to confront his past while chasing his future. But the gods would soon learn that Malazar was no one's jest. With a newfound determination set in his cold eyes, he prepared for what was to come.

"The game," he murmured to himself, the deadly whisper echoing around the room, "is afoot."

Chapter 22: Ascent into Danger

The winds at the base of Wind Heaven's Peak were already biting, howling ominously like ravenous wolves. It was a far cry from the sweltering heat of the desert, a complete turnaround that none of them had expected. The terrain was rocky and treacherous, each step requiring care and precision. Their task was to climb the mountain, yet it seemed the mountain had its own plans to stop them.

"Well, this is going to be a joyous hike," Joren muttered under his breath, tightening the straps of his pack. "Climbing a cursed mountain, facing mythical monsters, probably freezing our tails off. Can't wait."

"I'm glad to see your spirits remain high," Anwar chimed in, his voice thick with sarcasm. He glanced at the towering mountain before them, his usual joviality replaced by a steely determination.

"Wait till you see the ice golems," Kolos interjected, a knowing smirk playing on his lips. "They're like snowmen, but a tad bit more lethal."

"We're facing ice golems?" Lyra squeaked, eyes wide with surprise. Her pale face drained even more at Kolos's confirming nod.

"And you've faced these before?" Rafaela questioned, worry etching fine lines on her youthful face.

"Nah, but I've heard tales," Kolos replied nonchalantly. "Stories from Silverhand. Can't be that bad, right?"

Joren shook his head, finding some comfort in their shared apprehension. It was a grim comfort, but comfort nonetheless.

Their ascent began with a grueling pace, a steady rhythm that saw them making slow but significant progress. There were times when the wind threatened to blow them off their path, their steps skidding dangerously close to the edge. Every cliff they scaled, every monster they defeated, saw them inching closer to their goal.

First came the trolls, grotesque and as large as the boulders they hurled. They were slow but immensely strong, the force of their blows enough to shake the very ground beneath their feet. The fights were intense and bloody, their blows sending shockwaves rippling through the mountainside.

Next came the ice giants, towering behemoths of ice and snow, their icy breath chilling to the bone. The battles were brutal, the sheer power of the giants overwhelming. But with each victory, their confidence grew.

The ice golems proved to be the most challenging. Crafted from the very ice of the mountain, they were impervious to conventional attacks, their icy forms capable of regenerating almost instantly. But where strength failed, strategy prevailed.

Throughout their journey, they were tested to their limits, both physically and mentally. There were times when they felt the exhaustion threatening to engulf them, their bodies screaming for rest. But they pushed through, their resolve fueled by the thought of reaching the Oracle.

Mirages and illusions played tricks on their minds, showing them images of their deepest fears and desires. But they persevered, their bond growing stronger with each shared ordeal.

Laughter, however scarce, echoed through the mountain range, their shared humor a beacon of light in their treacherous journey. Their banter, sharp and light-hearted, helped alleviate the tension and keep spirits high.

By the end of the day, battered and weary, they set up camp, huddled together for warmth. Despite the hardship, they felt a sense of accomplishment. For the first time since they'd embarked on this journey, they truly felt like a team.

As the moon cast a serene glow on the mountain peak, they shared stories, their laughter and words intertwining with the howling wind. They were far from their goal, but for the first time, it seemed within their reach. A sense of camaraderie, born from shared struggles and victories, filled the air. They were ready to face whatever came next. For together, they knew they could conquer Wind Heaven's Peak.

Chapter 23: Whispers in the Shadows

The chill of the night had fallen over the mountainside, the once bright blues and whites of Wind Heaven's Peak replaced with dark hues of shadow and ice. The air hung heavy with a sense of anticipation, an icy edge that spoke of things hidden within the ancient crevices of the mountain.

They made camp at a relatively flat plateau, their bodies huddled together for warmth. Each of their breaths turned into small puffs of mist in the frosty air. The campfire flickered, casting dancing shadows that twisted and twirled around their makeshift camp.

From the depths of the dark, a whisper slithered through the night. It was soft, a mere caress against the howling wind, barely discernible but for those who were listening. A shiver ran down Joren's spine, the words curling around his senses like tendrils of frost.

"Did you guys hear that?" Joren asked, his voice hardly more than a whisper itself, betraying his unease.

Hearing Joren's words, Rafaela concentrated on the ambient sounds. Her empathic abilities enhanced her perception, allowing her to sense emotions and intentions. The whisper carried a sense of ancient pain, and a longing that tore at her heart.

"There's something out there," Rafaela said, her voice filled with concern, her hand tightening around her staff.

Their gazes darted around, peering into the darkness that blanketed the surrounding cliffs. The whispering voices grew louder, a chorus of unseen spirits that filled the night air with an eerie melody.

Anwar, usually jovial and cheerful, had a serious expression on his face. He had been trained to face all manner of creatures and foes, but spirits were another matter. He clasped his hands together in prayer, calling upon his god for protection.

The whispers seemed to react to Anwar's prayer,

the ethereal voices growing louder and more frantic. A cold wind swept through the campsite, causing the fire to flicker and cast erratic shadows against the icy backdrop.

In a moment of resolve, Anwar stood, his hands still clasped in prayer. The soft glow of holy light started to radiate from him, casting a warm aura around the group. His voice rang clear and strong in the still night, invoking a prayer of protection.

As Anwar's holy light spread, pushing back the oppressive shadows, the whispering spirits recoiled. The eerie voices receded, swallowed up by the vast expanse of the mountains.

Warmth filled the camp, the darkness and despair replaced by Anwar's aura of courage. His prayer brought solace to their hearts and stilled their trembling hands.

Anwar then went on, telling stories of bravery and hope to distract the group from the night's events. The sense of unease was slowly replaced by shared laughter and camaraderie, their spirits once again lifted.

Yet even as they rallied around Anwar's stories, they knew the trials of Wind Heaven's Peak were far from over. They needed to rest, regain their strength, and prepare for the climb that awaited them in the morrow.

As the fires burned low and their eyes grew heavy, they wrapped themselves in their cloaks, seeking the warmth and comfort of sleep. One by one, they drifted into dreams, the echoes of Anwar's prayers lulling them into a peaceful rest.

The climb up Wind Heaven's Peak was proving to be more daunting than they had ever imagined. Yet, they were determined, their spirits unyielding. They were a team, a beacon of hope against the mountain's chilling desolation. And nothing, not even the whispering spirits of the ancient mountain, could deter them from their path.

Chapter 24: Rogue's Guidance

In the monochrome realm of ice and snow, as blinding sunlight shimmered across the mountainscape, our heroes trudged on. The gnawing cold seeped into their bones, the biting wind cut through their armor, and the eerie silence hung heavy, making their spirits sag. Wind Heaven's Peak, with its sprawling icy canvas, was unyielding and treacherous.

Exhausted and growing increasingly disoriented, they realized they had been circling the same location over and over again. Kolos examined the environment, his arcane senses reaching out, but even his magic proved ineffective. Anwar, Rafaela, and Joren too were stumped, the featureless terrain providing no discernible landmarks. Their journey had come to a standstill.

"It's like being trapped in a labyrinth with no walls," Rafaela sighed, looking hopelessly around.

Anwar responded, "If only our path were lit by my Holy Light. But even it seems subdued in this relentless white wasteland."

They were on the verge of despair when they turned to Lyra, their agile rogue, who was eerily calm amidst the chaos. She'd been quiet, her gaze distant yet focused. A faint smile spread on her lips as she saw her friends turn to her with hope in their eyes. It was her time to shine.

"My friends, let me guide us. Trust in me." Lyra's voice was confident, echoing through the icy winds.

Suddenly, her HUD lit up with prompts:
-Scouting: Activated
-Hunt and Trail: Activated
-Heightened Senses: Activated
-Perception of the Hunter: Activated

She focused, relying on her heightened senses and perception. She scanned their surroundings carefully, but everything seemed uniform. Snow-covered rocks, ice-coated trees, unchanging sky. But her rogue instincts weren't convinced. She had learned to trust the invisible, to see what wasn't visible to the naked eye.

For hours, she led the group in various directions,
trusting her senses, believing in her instincts.
Joren, ever the skeptic, voiced his concern, "Are
we not just going around in circles again, Lyra?"
His words carried a hint of frustration, his patience
wearing thin.

Lyra replied, a hint of annoyance creeping into her
voice, "Joren, I can't show you a nicely paved road
or a shining beacon, alright? This isn't like hitting a
Harpy with your hammer. This is subtler, trickier. I
need you to trust me."

Joren nodded, muttering an apology, falling back
into step behind her. They all walked on, faith in
Lyra driving their steps, the bitter cold testing their
resolve.

Finally, just as doubts started creeping back in,
Lyra stopped abruptly. Her eyes focused on
something ahead. There it was. A subtle alteration
in the icy wind's direction, a slight disturbance in

the snow's uniformity, almost imperceptible, but to Lyra, it was as clear as day.

"This is it. This is our path," she declared, pointing towards an area that looked no different to the rest of the terrain.

Anwar squinted, "Are you certain, Lyra? There seems to be nothing."

"Yes, Anwar, I am. This is the path. I can sense it. Now, trust in me and walk."

Trust they did. Following their rogue, they marched on. It was a leap of faith, guided by nothing more than Lyra's senses. The journey was strenuous, their path invisible, and yet, they moved forward, driven by the hope that they were on the right path.

And then, as if a veil lifted, the terrain started to change subtly. A thin trail began to appear beneath the snow, winding its way up the mountainside. The treacherous, disorienting white landscape gradually gave way to clearer paths, rugged but visible. As they emerged from the white labyrinth, a collective sigh of relief echoed through the group.

Lyra's HUD lit up again, glowing with a gratifying message: Trial Passed – Trust in Instincts.

She looked back at her companions, grinning, "Told you."

Laughter erupted, echoing through the peak, a sweet sound in the cold, harsh mountain. The shared victory lifted their spirits, rekindling their resolve to press onward. The rogue had proved her mettle, and the journey was back on track. United, they pressed onward, ready to face whatever trials Wind Heaven's Peak had in store for them.

Chapter 25: Healer's Endurance

They had been trudging along the icy slopes for what felt like an eternity. The cold had long since burrowed into their marrow, and the biting wind made every step an ordeal. The hunger gnawing at their insides was a constant reminder of their dwindling resources.

Then, almost miraculously, a grove of lush, fruit-bearing trees sprung into their path. An oasis in the middle of their icy purgatory. Vibrant and tantalizing, the grove promised sweet, succulent relief from their desperate hunger.

Unthinking, the group rushed forward, driven by their raw, primal need. They plucked and devoured the fruits in a frenzy. Sweet juices dripped down their chins as they filled their bellies, their faces reflecting relief and joy.

Then, just as sudden as their salvation, came their damnation.

One by one, their bodies began to rebel. A blue-purple hue spread across their skin, their eyes became unfocused, and they convulsed in pain. Vivid hallucinations gripped their minds, and their cries echoed through the mountains.

Rafaela felt the poison coursing through her own veins, the pain shooting through her body. But as the party's healer, she was blessed with a higher poison resistance. Her mind remained somewhat clear amidst the tumultuous chaos.

Taking a deep breath, Rafaela activated her Healing aura. Light radiated from her, illuminating the darkening grove. Her HUD lit up with prompts, casting the status and health of each party member in sharp relief. They were poisoned and under the influence of a strong curse. Her job was cut out for her.

Rafaela began the arduous task of healing each member. She first tackled the hallucinations, projecting calming waves of holy energy into each of them. It required a delicate touch, a soothing approach that went against her instincts. They were in pain and she wanted to end it, but she had to be patient.

Next came the extraction of the poison. It was an excruciating process. She had to draw the poison from her friends into herself, the pain of the poison amplifying tenfold as it passed through her. She grunted, biting down on her lip, her body shaking with the effort. But she pushed through, neutralizing the poison with her holy energy and expelling it from her body.

Lastly, she had to break the curse. Her knowledge of the arcane was limited, but she had a basic understanding of curses. She poured her energy into dispelling the dark magic, the curse fighting back, attempting to latch onto her. But she resisted, pushing against it with all her might.

Finally, with the curse broken and the poison removed, she turned to restore their health. This was the easy part, something she was familiar with. But she was exhausted, her mana nearly depleted, and she had to force herself to continue.

One by one, she restored their health, watching as their health bars on her HUD filled up. The pain lessened, their breathing steadied, the hallucinations faded.

Rafaela finished with Joren. As she completed her healing, her HUD lit up once more: Trial Passed – Selfless Healing.

With that, Rafaela's strength gave out. She collapsed, her eyes fluttering shut. As she slipped into unconsciousness, she felt strong arms catch her, lowering her gently onto the snow. Soft murmurs of gratitude reached her ears as she succumbed to her exhaustion, knowing that she had done her duty. She had passed her test.

Chapter 26: Dance of the Arcane

Their trek up the icy mountains continued, their bodies sore and weary. Rafaela had recovered somewhat, her face pale, but her resolve unbroken. The road was harsh and unforgiving, but they forged ahead. And then, they came upon them - ethereal creatures woven from threads of pure arcane energy.

The party was quick to react, immediately assuming battle stances. They launched themselves at these strange beings, weapons slicing through the frigid air. But their attacks merely phased through the energy beings, leaving them untouched. Yet, they could feel the creatures' attacks, harsh and searing, like raw, untamed magic.

The party struggled, their attacks useless, their defenses crumbling. Kolos, however, was watching the whole event unfold with furrowed brows, deep in thought. He was quick to realize what they were facing. These were arcane refractions, spirits from the unseen arcane plane. They were untouchable, their essence weaving and bending through physical attacks. It was up to him to protect his friends from this ethereal threat.

His HUD sprung to life, showing him the grayed-out HP bars of the spirits, signifying their invulnerability. Their threat level was at an all-time high, but Kolos was not fazed. This was a trial he had been preparing for, knowingly or not.

Acting quickly, he lured the spirits away from his friends. He cast a barrage of arcane spells, each attack targeting the spirits' mana. He wasn't trying to hurt them, merely provoke them, lead them away from his team. And it worked. The spirits, enraged by the loss of mana, turned their attention solely to Kolos.

Now came the crucial part of his plan. He took a deep breath, focusing all his remaining energy into a single spell. "Arcane Isolation Pyramid!" he cried out. A pyramid of pure arcane energy erupted from the ground, enveloping Kolos and the spirits. The pyramid acted as an impenetrable barrier, sealing the spirits from the material world.

An intense fight ensued, the inside of the pyramid a spectacle of flashing lights and harsh cracks of energy. Kolos was on the defensive, dodging and countering the spirits' attacks as best as he could. But he was outnumbered, his strength dwindling rapidly.

Despite their desperation, his friends could do nothing but watch helplessly from outside the pyramid. They pounded against the arcane barrier, but it held firm. Kolos would not let it down, not when he knew what these spirits were capable of.

Throughout the whole ordeal, Kolos had been taking note of the spirits' mana bars, displayed on his HUD. He knew he could not defeat them in a battle of strength. But he had a different strategy. As he absorbed their arcane energy attacks, they were depleting their mana. Once he saw their mana bars drop low enough, he knew it was time to make his move.

With a shout that echoed through the mountains,

he cried out, "Domination of the Arcane!" His voice rang clear and firm, defying the chaotic dance of the arcane around him. This was his moment, his trial. The spirits, their mana depleted, had no means to defy him. After a moment of resistance, they succumbed, their forms solidifying as they fell under his command.

As the pyramid dispelled, Kolos collapsed, exhausted and battered. The arcane spirits hovered around him, their forms taking shape - an owl, a wolf, a horse. He weakly gestured at them, saying, "I release you from this realm, that you may go in peace into the unseen where you belong." They nodded, their forms dissipating into nothingness, leaving only the echo of gratitude behind.

As Kolos' eyes closed, his HUD came alive once again, Trial Passed - Master of the Arcane, it declared. He had passed his test. His friends rushed to his side, relief washing over them as they saw his faint, triumphant smile.

Chapter 27: Tales by the Fireside

As the sky darkened, their weary bodies finally settled down around the warmth of a crackling fire. Their path had been fraught with peril and danger so far, but tonight, the mountain offered them a respite. A stillness filled the air, a soothing balm that seeped into their bones and eased the lingering tension.

Seated in a rough circle around the fire, the party exchanged stories and laughs, their voices echoing off the mountainside. The firelight danced across their faces, casting long shadows that swayed with the night breeze.

Lyra, with her rogue's charm, told tales of daring exploits, her humor-filled narration bringing much-needed laughter. Anwar, in contrast, shared stories from his Holy Paladin trials, each tale a testament to his unwavering faith. Rafaela, shy but heartfelt, told them about her journey as a healer, her struggles, and her triumphs. Joren, usually stoic, let loose a few anecdotes of his blacksmithing days, each tale more astonishing than the last.

As the night wore on, Anwar turned to Kolos, curiosity twinkling in his eyes. "Kolos, how did you come to be Antonius Silverhand's apprentice? You've never shared that tale with us."

Kolos paused, his gaze distant as he gathered his thoughts. "It's a long story," he began, his voice a low hum against the crackling fire.

"First, I was a slave. That is until my master, the Baron of Daileem found out I had magical capabilities. So, he decided I'd be worth more as a curiosity, a mere circus freak to showcase for money. People paid to see me perform cheap tricks. It was humiliating." He paused for a second "But I managed to escape. One night as he came to feed me, I stabbed him in his throat with shards of ice I made from his own saliva. I'd had enough of that man. Then all I remember is running. Running until I couldn't feel my legs. Eventually I made it to Sadrym where I lived as an outcast. I was nothing more than a homeless boy. But at least I was free. Stealing was the only way I knew how to survive. One day, my theft was not just of bread, but of magic. I had managed to learn a few spells on my own and used them to steal from an old witch. It was some artifact; I barely remember what it was. All I remember is being hungry, so very hungry that day."

Kolos paused, his gaze unfocused as he relived his past. "Then, Antonius found me. He dragged me by the ear, took me back to the old lady, and made me return what I stole. He made me apologize."

A few chuckles rang out around the fire, picturing a young Kolos caught and dragged by the ear.

"I hated him, truly hated him at that moment," Kolos continued, a wry smile playing on his lips. "But, instead of handing me over to the authorities, he took me in. He fed me, clothed me, and showed me how to properly wield my magic. He turned my

114

life around. To me, he's more than just a mentor. He's the only father I've ever known."

Joren, who had been listening intently, asked, "So why don't you ever talk about him? We hardly knew of him until we were on our way to see him."

Kolos looked at Joren, his eyes reflecting the flickering firelight. He sighed and replied, "That, my friend, is a story for another day. For now, we should rest and gather our strength. The climb continues tomorrow, and we don't know what lies ahead."

With that, they each settled down, their eyes heavy with sleep. The fire burned lower, the sparks flying up to join the star-studded sky. Their bonds had deepened that night, their shared stories a testament to their camaraderie. They knew not what the future held, but they were ready to face it, together.

Chapter 28: The Chill of Resolve

Their journey continued ever upward, the climate growing ever more frigid as they scaled the mountain. Every breath became a puff of fog in the biting cold, while ice crystals formed on their lashes. Each step was a labor, as if they were dragging heavy chains through a knee-deep sea of snow.

Despite their resilience, the extreme cold began to take its toll. Hypothermia, a silent killer, began to creep upon them. One by one, the team members succumbed, collapsing into the snow, their bodies trembling from the relentless cold. Anwar, Lyra, Rafaela, Kolos, and finally, Joren too, fell into an eerie, painful sleep that flirted dangerously close to death.

Within the grips of this near-death slumber, Joren found himself adrift in a sea of memories. He saw the faces of his friends, heard laughter and cries, each memory an echo of their shared journey. His heart ached with the love he held for them. As these images whirled around him, a familiar voice called to him from the abyss.

Marylynn.

He followed the sound of her voice, a beacon in the tumultuous storm of his mind. His ethereal steps brought him back to his humble village, back to his forge, and back to Marylynn. Her face was as he remembered, warm and kind, her eyes filled with maternal love.

Tears welled in his eyes as he embraced her, the words falling from his lips in an urgent rush. "I've missed you so much. I'm sorry I wasn't there when you..."

"Shh," she soothed, her hand stroking his hair. "It's all right, my boy. I am so proud of you."

Her words echoed around him, a soothing balm against his guilt. He knew then, he had to return. His friends needed him. "But how?" he asked, feeling the warmth of her embrace fading, replaced by the chilling grasp of his reality.

"You never give up," Marylynn's voice echoed in his mind, her image fading as he was pulled back into consciousness.

Joren awoke with a gasp, his body rigid with cold. The chill had bitten deep into his flesh, numbing him to the core. But within him, a flame ignited. His resolve, his will to protect his friends, his promise to never give up, it all came crashing down upon him.

Closing his eyes, Joren let out a breath, allowing the heat within him to rise. The Flame of the Phoenix, that once small ember, now erupted in a blaze of brilliant blue fire. It spread, consuming him, spreading warmth into his frozen limbs.

With renewed vigor, Joren stood tall against the brutal cold. The blizzard seemed to quail before his determined gaze, the skies parting to reveal a sight of unimaginable beauty. A temple, glistening with precious stones, surrounded by flora and fauna untouched by time, stood majestically on the peak.

One by one, his friends stirred, their bodies thawing, their spirits lifted by the sight before them. They had made it to Wind Heaven's Peak, proving their worth against the trials thrown at them.

Joren's HUD came alive, the words glowing brilliantly against the serene backdrop. "New Ability Unlocked
Genesis: Dawn of the Phoenix."

Chapter 29: The Heart of Eternity

As they ventured forward into the heart of the ethereal realm at the summit of the mountain, their senses were inundated by the majestic grandeur and timeless beauty that surrounded them. Trees of opulent shades of green, their leaves shimmering with the hues of a forgotten rainbow, towered high, their branches heavy with ripe, tantalizing fruits that the world had long thought extinct.

Everywhere, flowers of an unimaginable variety bloomed, their petals an array of colors that danced in the vibrant sunlight. Rivers of crystal-clear water flowed like liquid silver, nourishing the lush vegetation and giving life to rare, beautiful creatures who roamed these sacred lands.

All around them were precious stones, glimmering diamonds, rubies, emeralds, and sapphires, strewn about as though left as an afterthought by nature, their facets catching the light and scattering it in a kaleidoscope of radiant colors. Great veins of gold and silver coursed through the rock faces, their luster as bright as the day they had been formed.

As they walked through this paradise lost to time, their eyes fell on magnificent wall carvings and ancient scriptures etched into stone tablets. These depicted a tale as old as time itself, a chronicle of the mighty dragons who had once graced the earth with their majestic presence. Their wings would eclipse the sun, their roars would shake the mountains, and their fire would light up the darkest corners of the world.

Yet, despite their overwhelming might, they were gone, fallen into the annals of history, their majesty, beauty, and power reduced to mere legends and lore. A melancholy descended upon the group, a deep sorrow for the creatures they had never known, but now felt an inexplicable connection to.

"And to think," Anwar murmured, his eyes

scanning the intricate carvings with reverence,
"only one remains. How lonely she must feel."

Their silent contemplation was broken by the
colossal temple doors, as grand and awe-inspiring
as the rest of the realm, made entirely of solid
emerald, etched with the legacy of the dragons. As
they approached, the doors began to move,
creaking open to reveal the hallowed halls within.
The sheer weight and size of the doors made the
very ground beneath their feet vibrate, the
resonance echoing in the pit of their stomachs.

As the doors opened, they were greeted with a
burst of warm, welcoming light. A gentle breeze
carried the fragrant scent of ancient incense, while
an unseen choir seemed to sing an age-old hymn,
the notes resounding in their very souls.

With awe-filled hearts, they stepped into the
temple, their breath hitching at the sight that
greeted them. Statues of dragons adorned the high
vaulted ceiling, their eyes glittering with
gemstones, their wings carved to depict a sky filled

with stars.

The time had come to meet the Oracle, the last of her kind. Their hearts pounded in their chests, a combination of excitement, fear, and an indescribable sense of reverence. The enormity of what lay before them was humbling, the echoes of the past whispering tales of grandeur, power, and melancholy into their eager ears.

And so, their journey led them onward, into the heart of the Dragon's realm, their footsteps echoing in the halls of antiquity, their story yet to be told, yet forever intertwined with the legacy of the Dragons. As they entered, they knew that they were stepping into a chapter of history that was meant for them and them alone, an intersection of destinies, the threshold of a timeless saga.

Chapter 30: The Voice of the Oracle

Through the grand emerald gates, the band of adventurers ventured, their footsteps echoing within the expansive hall of the temple. The space was dimly lit, save for the ethereal light that spilled from the open roof, casting long, dancing shadows on the intricately carved walls. The sight of the Oracle stirred the deepest parts of their hearts, a colossal figure sprawled across the altar in slumber, her scales glinting iridescent in the spilling moonlight.

She didn't react to their presence, but a slow sigh escaped her maw, shifting the air around them and signifying her awareness. The group remained hushed, the majesty of the Oracle silencing their voices. It was a solemn moment, and each member grappled with the magnitude of the presence they now stood before.

Yet, it was Joren who dared to break the silence. His heart pounding in his chest, he stepped forward, his voice carrying throughout the silent hall. "Great Oracle," he began, the words carrying an immense weight he'd never felt before. "We've journeyed far and faced trials we never imagined to stand here before you. We carry the hope of Aelloria on our shoulders, hope for a future where darkness no longer engulfs the light."

His words echoed in the vast chamber, lingering in the air before slowly fading away. He spoke of the struggle, the hardship they had endured, of the friends they had lost, his voice cracking ever so slightly as he recounted their journey.

Suddenly, the great Oracle stirred, her eyes opening to reveal endless pools of wisdom. Her voice filled the space, a deep rumbling that vibrated the air itself. "Speakst thou of struggle and loss, young Phoenix?" she queried in a tone that seemed to shake the very foundations of the temple. "What know'st thou of solitude and sorrow? What know'st thou of love lost and hearts left broken in the wake of time?"

The Oracle paused, her gaze penetrating Joren. "I have seen empires rise and fall, have witnessed the birth and death of stars. I have seen my kin vanish from existence, and the beauty of our kind fade from memory. I have borne the weight of millennia, have mourned the passing of those I cherished, and in my heart remains the echoes of their laughter and their cries of despair."

The Oracle's voice took a somber turn as she continued. "The Phoenix that slumbers within thee was a friend of old, a companion in a world long forgotten. Yet, now, it is bound within the confines of a human soul, an existence too small and fleeting to grasp the vastness of an immortal spirit."

She paused, eyeing Joren with an intensity that shook him to his core. "Tell me, boy, what canst thou say of love, of loss, of life? I have seen many come before thee, and one by one, they fell when the world needed them most. The shortcomings of thy kind have been the same throughout the ages - self-preservation, greed, selfishness."

Joren was left speechless at the Oracle's words, his heart pounding in his chest. A silence followed, heavy and profound, each of his companions in their thoughts. The Oracle's words were a harsh truth, a stark reminder of their duty and the weight they carried.

The room was filled with a long silence as Joren gathered his thoughts, his gaze never leaving the Oracle. This chapter was not the end, but the beginning of an even bigger challenge they had to face. It was a moment to reflect, to understand, and to stand steadfast in their resolution.

The Oracle had spoken, and they had listened. Now, it was time for them to respond. Their journey was far from over, and the Phoenix, even though quiet within Joren, was ready to rise once again.

***

Information for Public Disclosure
Game Lore:

In the annals of legend, there exists the Oracle, a being of immense wisdom and power, known across epochs by a myriad of titles. She is recognized as the "final dragon" of the ancient realm. In contemporary Aelloria, the line of dragons indeed endures, albeit in the diminished form of lesser drakes. These creatures, tamed and bred by humankind, are but a pale echo of their forebears, void of the gift of speech and bereft of higher intellect.

*Yet, in all significant regards, the Oracle, the magnificent White Queen of Wind Heaven's Peak, stands unchallenged, a timeless sentinel. In the echoes of the elder tales and the whispers of the wind, she is revered as the **"last"** true dragon of Aelloria. Her majesty and power are a testament to an era long gone, a stark reminder of the grandeur that once was and might never be again.*

Class: Deity
Level: Unspecified
Element/Affinity: Fire, Wind.
Unique Affinity: Time and Space
HP: ∞
Mana: ∞

Chapter 31: Words of Comrades

Silence. An unbearable silence hung heavy within the grand, emerald temple after the Oracle's profound words. Joren stood, rooted to the spot, the echoes of the Oracle's questions reverberating in his mind. He felt exposed and small, like a child facing the vast cosmos for the first time, grasping the magnitude of his insignificance.

It was not him, however, who broke the stillness. It was his friends, his comrades-in-arms, who stepped forward, their voices echoing in the vast chamber.

Anwar, the paladin whose youthful innocence was tempered by a wellspring of courage, stepped forward. His usual soft voice carried an unusual resolve. "Great Oracle, you've misjudged our friend. Joren isn't the ordinary man you perceive him to be," he stated with undeniable certainty, his words bouncing off the towering temple walls. "He carries the essence of an ancient spirit, yes. But he carries it with a resilience and honour that's entirely his own."

Next, from the temple shadows, Lyra stepped into the light, her face illuminated by the intricate glow from the carved walls. A mischievous glint played in her eye as she met the Oracle's gaze with defiance. "Joren is not one to turn tail and run from his fate. He stares it right in the eye," she affirmed, her tone brimming with pride and admiration. "He's faced pain and loss, yes, but he hasn't allowed these experiences to break him. Instead, he's used them to mould himself, to become stronger, to become the man he is today."

Following her words, Kolos found his courage. He stepped forth, the runic markings on his face and arms shimmering under the temple's gentle light. "Joren is more than just a carrier for the Phoenix," he stated firmly, his youthful voice ringing out with maturity and conviction. "He's our comrade, our brother. He's been there for us when we needed him, and we...we stand with him."

Rafaela, the delicate and empathetic healer of their group, was the last to raise her voice. Her words, soft and gentle, flowed like a soothing stream, but carried an unmistakable conviction. "Joren's heart is selfless and pure. He has risked his life countless times, for us and for those he doesn't even know, for a world that may not remember his sacrifice," she proclaimed, her green eyes welling up with emotion. "If that doesn't scream selflessness, then I don't know what does."

The chamber fell silent once more, their words hanging in the air, a testament to their faith in their friend. Their words were not just a defense but a declaration of their unwavering trust in Joren, their friend and comrade. The air within the temple seemed to stir, the Oracle's massive form shuffling as she considered their words.

Their heartfelt speeches touched her ancient, dragon heart. The Oracle's glowing eyes softened as she looked upon them, her voice rumbling as she responded.

"Verily, thou art defended by thine allies with such fervor and passion," she said, her voice echoing around the temple, "Yet, what thou seekest is not within the grasp of mere mortals. The flame that sleeps within thee, it is but a flicker against the raging storm that Malazar hath unleashed. The power he wields hath grown beyond my sight, casting shadows upon the threads of future, past, and present. Such darkness hath not been seen since the days of old when gods themselves battled against unspeakable evils."

She paused, her gaze falling upon the intricate mosaic floor of the temple. "Mayhap it is time the world faced the chaos that lies ahead. A tumultuous upheaval that even I, the last of my kind, cannot predict."

Joren, bolstered by his friends' words, stepped forward once more, the fire in his eyes glowing brighter. "Then let the world face it," he said, his voice ringing with determination, "For as long as we draw breath, we will not back down. We will stand against Malazar, against the chaos, and bring forth a dawn that Aelloria deserves."

The Oracle looked at him, her eyes glinting with something that seemed like respect. "Very well, young Phoenix Bearer," she said, a hint of a smile playing on her aged features. "Thou hast spoken thy piece with great conviction. I see now why the Phoenix hath chosen thee."

For a moment, it felt like the air in the temple stilled, anticipation hanging heavy. Then, with a slow nod of her massive head, the Oracle agreed, "Prepare thyself, for the trials that lie ahead are beyond any thou hast faced till now."

The path ahead was fraught with dangers unknown, their future uncertain. But with the Oracle's wisdom to guide them, and their unyielding conviction in each other, the young heroes stood ready to face whatever lay ahead, bound by a shared destiny and the promise of a dawn yet unseen.

Chapter 32: The Echoes of Aelloria

Our young heroes stood within the grand cavern of the Oracle's sanctum, enveloped in a quietude that echoed with countless epochs. The Oracle, an immense figure wreathed in the time-worn wisdom of myriad centuries, surveyed them with an inscrutable gaze.

"Attend well, young ones, and take to heart the tale I speak, for it is of dread import," the Oracle began, her voice a deep, sonorous roll that vibrated through the expansive sanctum. "It is a tale of the Deathreaver Scepter, a creation of such fell power that its existence breeds a terror that blights the hearts of the brave."

Her utterance was ponderous, each word pronounced with a gravity that underscored the magnitude of the narrative. "The scepter commands an authority that defies comprehension,

God-slayer it is known, and armed with such a tool, Malazar challenges the celestial court in its entirety."

As the Oracle's words resonated within the chamber, a frigid hush crept amongst the gathering, chilling the marrow of their bones. The horror was palpable, a testament to the potency of the dread weapon.

"Your valour and unity light the frost within my ancient heart, yet I do caution that bravery alone will not see thee through the trials to come. To seek combat now will but secure your doom and forestall the Phoenix's re-emergence by a century," she counselled. Her gaze was tinged with an ineffable sadness.

"Forsooth, Aelloria will not await the Phoenix. The world you cherish will be but an echo of its former self, if indeed it survives."

As her declaration hung heavy in the air, Anwar found his voice, his determination resounding clear. "Oracle, pray tell us, what must we do?"

Summoning her strength, the Oracle rose, her grand form framed by the temple's austere beauty. "Walk with me, children. 'Tis time for a parting gift."

Deeper into the temple they ventured, the Oracle's voice a guiding beacon in the shadows. "Even mine own foresight, once clear as a crystal stream, is now clouded, shrouded by a darkness I cannot pierce. Yet, within this darkness, thy valiant hearts shine, illuminating the murk with your thirst for justice and the luminescence of thy fellowship."

"We stand at the twilight of the gods, yet a flicker of hope remains. A future may yet be salvaged, wherein our world endures."

Upon reaching the sanctum's core, the Oracle, with a whispered sigh, shed a scale, an iridescent shard that danced with celestial light. "Take this, noble hearts," she said resonating with the weight of her sacrifice. "With mine own scales, may thou find the fortitude needed for the trials that lie before thee."

As they each accepted a fragment of the Oracle's essence, a sense of unity and resolve bound them. Each held the scale, feeling its vibrancy resonate with their individual spirits, a symbol of the ancient dragon's trust and hope. And then, a tremor. The earth beneath them shook violently as a sound, distant yet powerful, echoed through the temple. The Oracle, with a look of surprise and fear, whispered, "We are too late. The God-killer awakens..." The temple shook again, this time with more force, and the once-sturdy walls began to crumble...

And thus, our heroes, under the chilling omen of impending doom, stood at the precipice of an epoch-ending battle.

Chapter 33: Of Ancient Scales and Looming Shadows

The tremors coursing through the temple's bones served as a dire herald, an insistent thrumming echoing the Oracle's grim foretelling. Their HUDs flickered, a sharp contrast to the dimly lit recesses of the dragon's lair, and suddenly, a message emblazoned across their field of vision: "Item Received: Scales of the Oracle."

The description unfurled beneath the item's moniker. "Scales of the mighty Oracle, first and last dragon of Aelloria. Power Level: Unspecified. Item Tier: Legendary, Deity. Item Use: Infuse essence on main weapon. Level required to use Item: 100 and above."

A collective gasp echoed in the cavernous depths of the sanctuary, their voices a meek chorus against the roiling tremors. They exchanged wide-eyed glances, the sheer power of their gifts not lost on them. A sense of awe, of reverence, filled their hearts.

"But we are but at level fifty-seven," Joren voiced the group's collective worry. "To reach level one hundred... it might take an age. How are we to utilize these?"

The Oracle, her ancient eyes glinting with determination, shook her massive head. "Indeed, thou art not yet prepared to harness mine essence. Yet despair not, brave souls. The time shall come when thou art ready, but for now, haste is thy greatest ally."

The Oracle's scales shimmered with a radiance that outshone the trembling cavern. "Thou must seek refuge with Antonius Silverhand. 'Tis he who holds his ground against the approaching storm. Malazar still fears him, and for good reason. He will shield thee, guide thee, as the realms rally to his call."

"Thou must make haste," she continued, her voice filled with a profound sorrow. "For the barriers of this sanctuary, held for eons by my magic, now wane under Malazar's relentless assault. I can delay him but not halt his onslaught."

Joren's face hardened, his eyes mirroring the burning resolve that stirred within his heart. "No, we won't leave you. We'll stay, fight with you."

His declaration echoed in the confines of the cavernous chamber, his friends nodding in agreement. Yet before any could further the sentiment, the Oracle interjected, "Nay, brave warrior. Thou must..."

But her words trailed off, drowned by a booming crash. The tremors intensified, a cacophony of shifting stones and trembling earth. An ominous rumble filled the cavern, drowning their words, their thoughts, their promises.

Chapter 34: A Farewell in Time

The dragon's command echoed within the chamber, resonating with the pulsing tremors that shook the temple's ancient bones. They would need to leave, to run, but the idea of leaving the last dragon of Aelloria to face her inevitable doom alone tugged painfully at their hearts.

The Oracle, steadfast in her resolve, sliced through reality with a colossal claw. A swirling, shimmering portal unfurled in the wake of her action, a doorway leading away from the mountain, a passage to safety. "Thou must cross this rift, a haven in the folds of space and time," she commanded, her voice still strong and steady, an unwavering rock amidst the turbulent quaking.

Biting his lip, Anwar turned to the Oracle, his heart heavy with sorrow. "What will become of you, Great Oracle?" His voice wavered, brimming with the turmoil of impending loss.

The Oracle, majestic and somber in her twilight moments, regarded him with a thoughtful gaze. "E'en in mine omniscience, 'tis a veil that shrouds the specter of death. A fate unforeseen, a future unsighted. My vision is clouded, dear boy, and thus I must face the unknown, as thou and all mortals must in time."

Her answer, indirect yet stark, unveiled the harsh reality they would have to accept. A great sense of melancholy washed over them, punctuated by the eerie silence that accompanied the sudden lull in the shaking.

Kolos, known for his humor and quick wit, dropped to his knees, an uncharacteristic seriousness reflecting in his eyes. "Your sacrifice will not be forgotten, Great Oracle. The stories of your majesty, the tales of your might, the legends of the last dragon of Aelloria... they will live on. I swear it."

His words hung in the air, a promise echoing amidst the mounting dread and urgency. A tribute to the soon-to-be fallen.

The Oracle's luminous gaze met Kolos', a touch of fondness softening her stern countenance. "'Fore the sun first took its place in the sky, I wandered these barren lands," she began, her voice taking on a far-off quality as she delved into the tales of a time long forgotten. "No life stirred, no breath rustled the leaves. A world untouched, unspoiled. I have seen the dawn of all things, and now, I shall greet the dusk with open wings."

Her admission, laced with an odd sense of peace, stilled the atmosphere. An air of sorrow blanketed the chamber, yet beneath it was a glimmer of resolve, of determination.

"Do not mourn my passing, children. Do not let sorrow cloud thy hearts," the Oracle implored, her gaze encompassing them all, bestowing upon them a silent strength. "For 'tis with willing steps that I stride into my end, eager to find solace in the everlasting sleep."

Her words, laden with a profound wisdom and acceptance, offered them a strange solace. Despite the pain that etched itself into their hearts, they nodded, understanding the magnitude of her sacrifice.

"Go now, dear ones. I shall watch over thee from the stars, my spirit ever with you. Rejoice, for the light of hope remains."

With her final blessing and a shared glance among them, our heroes stepped into the portal. They dared not look back, lest their resolve crumble. The rift closed behind them, leaving them with the resonating echo of the Oracle's words and a profound sense of loss, but also a resolute determination.

They were the last to have seen, to have spoken with, the last dragon of Aelloria. And now, they bore the weight of her hopes, her faith, upon their shoulders. The sorrow in their hearts was palpable, but so too was the spark of resolve, for they would honor the Oracle's sacrifice, they would save their home, or die trying.

Chapter 35: Clash of Titans

With a burst of foul magic, the last remnants of the protective barrier shattered, and Malazar, Lord of the Dead, stepped into the sacred heart of Wind Heaven's Peak. Each stride he took carried an unholy power that sent a wave of decay and corruption snaking across the ancient stone. The massive doors, wrought from the emerald-green stone of the mountain itself, swung open to his touch, their loud groan a grim harbinger of the confrontation to come.

Inside the grand sanctuary, the Oracle waited, her form bathed in the soft luminescence emanating from the altar. Unmoved by Malazar's entrance, she reared her majestic head and let out a thunderous roar that echoed through the chamber, the sound carrying a warning of the danger that awaited him.

"Thou art indeed mad, Malazar, to set foot within a

dragon's den uninvited, and a God's sanctuary at that!" she bellowed, her voice filling the cavernous space. It was a powerful and chilling reminder of her dominion over this place.

Malazar, unphased by the dragon's words, strode forward. His skeletal fingers closed around the hilt of the Deathreaver Scepter, its ominous glow casting an unsettling shadow over his skeletal features. "And what of gods, dear Oracle, when one wields a god-killer?" he retorted, his voice smooth and vile, like oil over a rotting carcass.

Their exchange was as cold and harsh as the icy winds that howled outside the mountain's peak, their words sparking with an intensity that could rival the raging storm outside. There was no love lost between them, and in the icy silence that followed their heated exchange, a menacing undercurrent thrummed, biding its time for the coming clash.

"You harbor the Phoenix Warrior," Malazar accused, his voice cutting through the frigid air.

His eyes, voids of endless darkness, were relentless and scrutinizing as they bore into the Oracle.

Undeterred by his accusatory tone, the Oracle responded with a poise befitting her divine status. "As a deity of the ancient world, I answer not to a vile serpent who deems himself a god merely by wielding forbidden magics," she retorted, her voice firm and unwavering. Her luminous eyes met his hollow gaze, the fire within them dancing with a challenge. "So come, if thou art here to slay me. Deemest thou me so defenseless? Let us put that to the test."

Malazar responded to her challenge with a cruel smile in morbid amusement, his skeletal fingers tightening around the scepter. "As you wish, your majesty," he responded, his voice echoing within the sacred chamber.

The showdown was imminent. The Oracle, an ancient god, and Malazar, the harbinger of death armed with a god-killer, faced each other, an undeniable tension radiating between them. This was no longer just a battle for survival, but a clash of titans, the turning point of an era.

As the two titans squared off, an ominous silence enveloped the sanctuary, a calm before the inevitable storm. The echoes of their exchange seemed to hang in the air, the tension palpable, the anticipation almost unbearable. The ensuing battle would determine the fate of Aelloria, for better or for worse.

And so, with a crackling burst of malicious energy from Malazar's scepter and a resonating roar from the Oracle, the clash of titans began.

Chapter 36: Clash of Titans, Part II

The thunderous heart of Wind Heaven's Peak was thrumming with a primal energy, an ancient power that had been held in balance for millennia. Yet now, that equilibrium was teetering on the edge of a precipice, as two colossal forces readied themselves for the coming storm. The Oracle, a celestial being of inimitable grace and power, stood tall and resolute in the heart of her sanctuary, her every breath echoing with the wisdom of ages past. Across from her, an entity of darkness and decay, Malazar, reeking of death and brandishing his god-killing scepter, his every movement a shadowy blur of malignant intent.

An unsettling silence hung over the sanctuary, a momentary lull before the impending tempest. Then, in a fraction of a second, the air was rent by the raw force of Malazar's spell, a surge of black energy that snaked its way towards the Oracle with an intensity that could shatter the very bedrock of the mountain. The Oracle responded, her eyes glimmering with an ancient fury, her tail swishing with a grace that belied its tremendous strength. With a single mighty sweep, she batted away the onslaught, her counterforce of wind creating a gust that stopped the spell in its tracks. The collision of the two opposing energies erupted in a dazzling explosion of light and sound, hurling ancient stone in a torrential downpour.

"Thou art a blight, Malazar," the Oracle roared, her voice reverberating in the cavernous depths of the sanctuary, "a poisonous worm gnawing at the roots of Aelloria!"

Malazar, not a creature to be daunted, responded with a ghastly laugh that echoed through the chamber like the rattle of dry bones in the wind. He lifted his scepter high, gathering another wave of necrotic energy that he flung towards the majestic dragon. "And you are an antiquated relic, clinging onto a world that has long forsaken you!"

Yet the Oracle was undeterred. As the surge of
decay bore down on her, she summoned an ancient
magic of her own, calling forth the primordial fire
that had danced in the bellies of the first dragons.
A wall of flame roared to life before her, colliding
with Malazar's spell in a mesmerizing display of
magic. Her words, punctuated by the crackling
fire, rang out with unyielding defiance, "I remain a
beacon of hope, a stalwart bulwark against
parasites such as thee!"

A symphony of power reverberated throughout the
sacred sanctuary, as fire clashed with decay, life
met death, and the echoes of their age-old rivalry
rang out in a guttural melody of war. Their battle
was as much a clash of ideologies as it was a
contest of raw power. On one side, the Oracle,
venerable and mighty, wielding the ancestral
flames of the dragons of old, stood as the
embodiment of the primal forces of nature. On the
other, Malazar, a symbol of death and decay,
brandished his unholy scepter, epitomizing the
destructive power of ambition and hubris.

In the sacred heart of the mountain, beneath the watchful gaze of forgotten deities immortalized in ancient stone, the very pillars of creation trembled under their strength. The outcome of their confrontation was as of yet uncertain, but one thing was clear: the ensuing chapters of this saga would be written in the ashes and embers of this cataclysmic duel, a testament to the titanic struggle between good and evil, between hope and despair.

Chapter 37: The Last Dragon's Fall

The colossal clash between the Oracle and Malazar echoed through Wind Heaven's Peak, a symphony of cataclysmic proportions. The sheer intensity of their duel was something hitherto unseen, a sight both awe-inspiring and terrifying. And within this tempest of divine wrath, a turning point was looming, waiting to break free.

Their powers clashed, a stunning dance of celestial fire and necrotic darkness. Yet, amidst this apocalyptic confrontation, Malazar's wicked grin widened. He raised his Deathreaver Scepter, and the room plunged into a chilling, spectral darkness.

"The tide of battle turns, and you are on the precipice of doom."

He swung his scepter, releasing an overwhelming wave of darkness and decay. The Oracle tried to counter, to rebuff the dark magic as she had been doing, yet the tide of necrotic energy was too great. It crashed onto her, a tsunami of death and decay, and for the first time, the Oracle faltered. The sea of darkness engulfed her, extinguishing her celestial flames.

The Oracle fell, her majestic form collapsing to the ground amidst a shower of sparks. Her moans of agony echoed through the halls of the sanctuary, a haunting testament to her grim plight. But even in her anguish, her spirit was not broken.

"Thou mayst stand tall now, Malazar, yet thou art a shadow, a pale imitation of true power," she managed, her voice filled with pain, but also with defiance. "Aelloria will resist thee, even unto her last breath. Thy victory will be but a fleeting illusion."

Malazar approached, his footsteps a hollow echo in the desolate sanctuary. "Illusion, Oracle? I think not," he sneered, his eyes gleaming with malicious delight. "Behold, the dawn of a new age begins with your demise!"

The Oracle, even in her downfall, held her head high, her eyes piercing Malazar's own. "Thy reign... will be but a chapter... in Aelloria's grand tale..."

As Malazar loomed over her, his scepter poised for the final blow, the Oracle's eyes shone brightly. Fearless. Defiant. Even in the face of her imminent end, the last Dragon of Aelloria held onto her dignity, her resolve, and her belief in the enduring spirit of her beloved land.

Malazar's wicked laughter echoed through the hollows of the sanctuary, a horrifying prelude to the final act in this epic clash.

Chapter 38: The Fall of a God, The Rise of Heroes

Joren dropped to his knees abruptly, his features distorted by a profound agony that rippled across his strong form. A shocked gasp escaped from his lips, a sound that echoed with a despair so profound that it stilled the world around them.

"She's dead..." he uttered through gritted teeth, clenching his fists in impotent rage. "He killed her."

Lyra rushed to his side, her eyes wide with alarm. "Joren!" she cried, her hands reaching out to steady him. Her mind was a whirlwind, her heart aching as she tried to comprehend the magnitude of what he'd just said. The Oracle, the last Dragon of Aelloria, was gone.

The enormity of the news took the breath from their lungs. A silence, heavy and suffocating, settled over the group. Rafaela wept openly, her emerald eyes filled with a despair that reflected the gloom that had descended upon them. Kolos held her close, a silent pillar amidst the storm of their shared grief.

Anwar, the holy paladin, stood tall, his eyes
glistening with unshed tears. He looked at his
friends, his comrades in arms, their spirits crushed
under the weight of their loss.

"She did not die in vain," Anwar began, his voice
strong and resonant despite his grief. His gaze
shifted to each of them, acknowledging their pain
but also their resolve. "The Oracle... she made a
choice. A choice to protect us, to protect Aelloria.
It's a choice we must honor."

His gaze lingered on Joren, a shared understanding
passing between them. "She saw something in us.
A chance to stand against the darkness. We owe it
to her, to ourselves, and to Aelloria to see this
through."

Lyra tightened her grip around Joren, her fingers
tracing soothing patterns on his back. Her eyes met
Anwar's, her determination reflecting his own.
"We will," she said, her voice steady. "We won't
let her sacrifice be in vain."

Rafaela nodded through her tears, her grip on Kolos' arm tightening. The mage gave a determined nod, the humor gone from his face, replaced by a solemn resolve. "For Aelloria," he affirmed, his voice carrying a strength that was as surprising as it was inspiring.

Anwar turned his gaze skywards, as if trying to catch a glimpse of the fallen Oracle among the stars. "For Aelloria," he echoed, his words hanging in the air like a sacred vow.

As they rose, their hearts heavy but their spirits ignited with a newfound determination, the first light of dawn began to breach the horizon, illuminating their path. It was as if the Oracle herself was guiding them, her radiant memory casting out the darkness.

Their journey was far from over, their hearts heavy with the weight of their loss. Yet, in the midst of their grief, a spark of hope ignited within them, fanned into flame by their shared determination.

The Oracle had bestowed upon them her final gift, her unyielding belief in their potential. And they would not let her down.

With a firm grasp, Joren drew forth the iridescent dragon scale, its majestic glow bathing his face in an ethereal light. His eyes, usually simmering with sorrow, now flickered with a new flame - a flame of fury.

"He has killed a God," he declared. The weight of his statement hanging heavy in the air. "If I am to bring him down... I must rise above the strength of the gods themselves."

Epilogue: The Last Breath of an Ancient God

Falling.

***

The world slowed to a crawl as the Last Dragon, the Oracle of Aelloria, teetered on the precipice of oblivion. The ground beneath her mighty form trembled, her heart echoed a slow, laborious drumbeat against her ribs. But in the belly of this monstrous despair, a spark flickered, a warmth that danced along her very bones.

To be held at the mercy of the very darkness she had foretold. Malazar, the bearer of the Deathreaver Scepter, stood above her, his smirk colder than winter's bite. But as the shadow of death fell over her, a radiant light shimmered into view. A hand, luminous and ethereal, emerged from the void, its touch gentle upon her snout.

"Oh, great maker," she breathed, her voice hushed and reverent. "Thy servant hath served thee well, but now, the curtain falls on the age of gods. To thee, I offer my last breath, my final thought."

Her eyes, a pair of glistening emerald pools, gleamed with defiance, her spirit still aflame. As her sight dimmed, and Malazar's victory drew near, a blinding flash consumed her form. Her soul, unfettered from the mortal coil, soared high, higher than the highest peaks of Aelloria, to the realm of the celestial bodies.

As she ascended, the firmament shone brighter, welcoming its lost kin. Once more she saw them, her fallen brethren, their celestial forms glittering like a bed of diamonds scattered across the velvet canvas of the sky. Their absence was a void she had carried within her for an eternity, and now, a sweet reunion awaited.

"Mine kin, I cometh home," she whispered, her voice echoing across the starlit sky.

She looked down upon the realm she had safeguarded for countless lifetimes. Aelloria, a world teetering on the brink of despair and hope. In the heart of this chaos, a beacon of light flared, the Phoenix warrior and his loyal companions.

Her eyes welled with a serenity that reflected the tranquility of the cosmos. She saw them not as they were, but as they could be, their potential limitless as the expanse of the universe.

"Fear not, children of Aelloria. The flame of hope burns bright within thee," she murmured, her voice imbued with the wisdom of the ages. "Let my fall be thy rise, rise and save our beloved realm. The time of the Gods hath ended, and in its stead, the age of heroes begins."

The Oracle's star shone brighter than any other, her light dancing across the sky, casting away the darkness. Her voice echoed across the universe, a promise, a prophecy. The tale of Aelloria was far from over.

Her spirit now one with the cosmos, the Oracle
found peace. An age ended, another began. Yet,
the songs of the Dragonkind would echo in the
winds of Aelloria, their legacy entrusted to the
Phoenix warrior and his comrades.

In death, as in life, the Oracle's voice echoed
through time, a testament to her wisdom, her
courage, her sacrifice. She may have fallen, but her
hope, her belief in the Phoenix warrior, and the
future of Aelloria, endured.

The story continues in Book III of the
Eternal Grind:

Echoes of the Phoenix Twilight

Available Now

Thank you for reading.

To receive emails regarding upcoming book deals, free book giveaways and updates on release dates sign up at:

https://joelpoe.com/contact/

Consider sharing your experience on Amazon. Reviews and ratings from readers like you help new readers find this story.

Till next time,

Joel Poe

Joel Poe

Printed in Great Britain
by Amazon

40761727R00106